Advance Praise for *All My Stripes*

"I've always felt that the teachers among us are real-life superheroes. And one important lesson they teach is that we should embrace the things that make each of us different and unique—whether it's having been bitten by a radioactive spider, turning green from gamma rays, or being born a zebra with a red autism stripe!

To the world at large, autism is still a mystery. That mystery vanishes as we lose our hearts to that wonderful, colorfully-striped zebra in a story so compelling you'll remember it always.

Reading specialist Shaina Rudolph and teacher Danielle Royer in their first children's book, lavishly illustrated by Jennifer Zivoin, bring this important lesson home not only to kids with autism and their siblings and classmates, but also to the world at large to whom autism is yet a mystery.

It teaches us to embrace not only who we are, but also to embrace the people around us who are brilliantly different thanks to their own amazing, colorful stripes."

—Stan Lee
Chairman emeritus of Marvel Comics and chairman of POW! Entertainment, co-creator of Spider-Man, the X-Men, the Fantastic Four, Iron Man, and the Hulk

"Shaina Rudolph and Danielle Royer have done a magnificent job shedding light on some of the hardships a child with autism goes through. Beyond this, they've done an equally impressive job detailing how unique, beautiful, and caring these children are. Zane is a hero in my eyes, just like each and every child out there dealing with autism. Additionally, Zane's Mama is a wonderful role model for parents and teachers and exemplifies a favorite quote of mine: 'With great love, all things are possible.'"

—Russell Simmons
Philanthropist and founder of Def Jam Recordings

"*All My Stripes* is a wonderful book that will delight children and parents alike. Entertaining, enjoyable, and enlightening."

—Bill Paxton
Emmy-nominated actor and director

"As the parent of a 27-year-old child with autism, I only wish *All My Stripes* had been around when my daughter was at a young age as it would have been yet another useful tool for us as parents, for her as a child, and for the rest of the world that she is now a part of."

—Joe Mantegna
Emmy-nominated actor and director

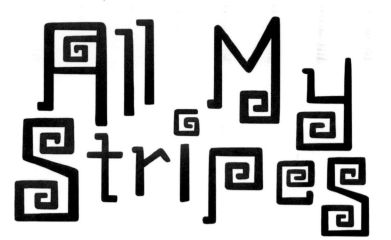

All My Stripes

A Story for
Children With Autism

by Shaina Rudolph and Danielle Royer
illustrated by Jennifer Zivoin

foreword by Alison Singer, President, Autism Science Foundation

MAGINATION PRESS · WASHINGTON, DC
American Psychological Association

To David, Mom, Dad, and all those with their own unique stripes who helped me find mine. As Oscar Wilde said: "Be yourself; everyone else is already taken."—*SR*

For my brothers and students, my truest inspirations.—*DR*

To my family, for your love and support of my artistic stripe—*JZ*

Published by
MAGINATION PRESS
An Educational Publishing Foundation Book
American Psychological Association
750 First Street, NE
Washington, DC 20002

For more information about our books, including a complete catalog, please write to us, call 1-800-374-2721, or visit our website at www.apa.org/pubs/magination.

Printed by Worzalla, Stevens Point, WI
Book design by Sue White

Library of Congress Cataloging-in-Publication Data
Rudolph, Shaina.
All my stripes : a story for children with autism / by Shaina Rudolph and Danielle Royer ; illustrated by Jennifer Zivoin.
pages cm
"American Psychological Association."
Summary: Zane rushes home to tell his mother about problems he faced during his school day, and she reminds him that while others may only see his "autism stripe," he has stripes for honesty, caring, and much more.
ISBN 978-1-4338-1916-2 (hardcover) — ISBN 1-4338-1916-3 (hardcover) —
ISBN 978-1-4338-1917-9 (pbk.) — ISBN 1-4338-1917-1 (pbk.)
[1. Autism. 2. Self-acceptance—Fiction. 3. Schools—Fiction.
4. Mothers and sons—Fiction. 5. Zebras—Fiction.] I. Royer,
Danielle. II. Zivoin, Jennifer, illustrator.
III. Title.
PZ7.R83All 2014
[E]—dc23   2014030924

Manufactured in the United States of America
First printing October 2014
10 9

One in 68 children is diagnosed with autism spectrum disorder. This means that just about everyone knows someone who is autistic.

Children with autism often feel different from their peers and don't always understand why. *All My Stripes* is the story of Zane, a young zebra with autism, who fears that his differences make him stand out from other children. With careful guidance from his mother, Zane learns that autism is only one of many qualities that make him special. *All My Stripes* is an important story because it teaches us that sometimes all it takes is a good look in the mirror to remember that each of us has important and unique gifts to offer the world.

All My Stripes is an excellent teaching tool for parents and educators who can help children understand that while their peers with autism may act differently, they still have plenty to offer. Children who read *All My Stripes* will learn to empathize with Zane and will take important lessons from this story back to their classrooms, making school a more welcoming place for everyone.

Alison Singer
President, Autism Science Foundation

Zane ran home as fast as he could.

"Nobody gets me, Mama!"

Mama hugged Zane. He began to tell her about his bad day.

"This morning in art class, the teacher started a hoof-painting project. I didn't want to get paint on my hooves, so the teacher gave me a paintbrush. All the other zebras noticed and were making fun of me because they didn't understand why I wouldn't use my hooves."

Mama said, "I bet that made you feel different from the rest of the group."

Zane replied, "It did, but paint is just too weird to touch.

During math class, the fire alarm blared loudly. While the children in my class were getting in line quietly, I hid under the desk screaming and covering my ears. The class left without me, and I was scared until the firefighters found me."

"When the class came back from lunch, everyone was putting their lunchboxes in their cubbies. Some classmates were talking about a video game I play all the time, but I didn't know how to start talking to them."

"I started talking about all the things I knew about the game, but since I was staring at the floor, nobody knew I was talking to them.

When the other kids walked away, I started talking louder. I really wanted them to hear me, but everybody was getting ready for science class."

"We sat down for science and were learning about the planets. Our teacher gave us each a planet to draw, but I wanted to create my own. When it came time to present, I felt different from the rest of the class again. My teacher loved my planet and said, 'Whatever floats your boat.'

"I spent the rest of the afternoon looking for a boat in the classroom."

Zane was crying.
"How come all anyone sees
is my **autism stripe**?!"

Mama carried Zane over
to the mirror. "When I look
at you, I see many different
stripes. If one of them were
missing, you wouldn't be
the same."

"I see your **pilot stripe**.
When we get lost
in the city,

you always remember
the way home."

"Your **caring stripe** makes you act kindly toward others. When your classmates think it's funny to bully other kids, you come to the rescue."

"Your **honesty stripe** lets me always trust
your word. When other parents have to worry
that their kids aren't telling the truth,
I know you always are."

"My favorite stripe is your **curiosity stripe**. When all the other kids are falling asleep in class, you always want to know more. I love when you come home and tell me everything you learned.

Sometimes you ask me questions and I don't even know the answers!"

Mama pointed out the rest of Zane's amazing stripes. The more stripes she explained, the better Zane began to feel about himself. By the time she was finished, Zane loved himself again.

Zane ran outside, feeling the warmth of the sun. Finally, he felt proud of all his stripes. He said, "There's more to me than just my autism stripe. It's just part of me. The other parts make the whole me. I love each stripe because without them, I wouldn't be me!"

Reading Guide

by Drew C. Coman, PhD, and Ellen Braaten, PhD

As a parent, it can be devastating when your child comes home from school distressed, anxious, and angry because he feels he has no friends or is misunderstood by his peers and teachers. For children on the autism spectrum, these days can be almost a daily occurrence, making life continually difficult for you and the rest of the family. In *All My Stripes*, Zane's "bad day" might sound familiar to you, but you may still be perplexed as to why this is such a frequent occurrence and what these behaviors might mean. This reading guide is offered as a way to further your understanding as to why these days occur and to give you some insight into how to cope with them. For an explanation of Zane's experienced challenges and even more importantly his strengths, as well as more information about autism spectrum disorders (ASD), please read on.

Being Different: "Nobody gets me, Mama!"

In the beginning of the story, Zane runs home as fast as he can and immediately seeks comfort from his mother as he reports, "Nobody gets me, Mama!" Navigating the social world is a universal struggle for children on the autism spectrum; it is considered one of the hallmark symptoms of the disorder. Children with ASD often understand, process, and interact with the world differently: sometimes for the better, sometimes in ways that make life more challenging, and sometimes simply differently. As the name "spectrum" implies, there are countless levels and differences in challenges experienced by each and every affected child. While Zane is experiencing challenges relating well to his peers, he is self-aware enough to identify his weakness with social relationships on his own. As such, Zane's symptoms would be considered "mild" given he is more in tune with his social weaknesses. However, even kids with more severe symptoms feel misunder-

stood and "out of sync" with their peers. While these symptoms are a source of stress for Zane, his insightfulness to these challenges—a clear strength—allows him to identify when things go awry when interacting with his peers. With appropriate supports in place and perhaps social skills training, he could learn some strategies to improve these abilities in the future.

Sensory Processing Challenges: "Paint is just too weird to touch"

In this story, Zane experiences sensory processing difficulties. Sensory processing challenges occur when a child is overly sensitive (hypersensitive) to things such as noise, sounds, foods, smells, and textures, or not sensitive enough (hyposensitive) to the point where he seems oblivious to things that would normally bother other kids. These kinds of difficulties are quite common in kids with ASD. For example, Zane does not like the feel of paint on his hooves, and he experiences an overwhelming sensation when the fire alarm goes off at school. These sensitivities can cause kids with ASD to have difficulty completing certain tasks, paying attention, or relating with peers who may not understand their behaviors. Something as simple as finger painting (or in Zane's case, hoof painting), or a loud noise, can lead to a downward spiral of negative events for children on the autism spectrum as it did for Zane. This is why occupational therapy that includes treatment for sensory problems is helpful for many with ASD.

Socio-Communicative Challenges: "I didn't know how to start talking to them"

Zane did not know how to initiate social interactions and communicate well with his classmates. While he was able to pick up on the fact his classmates were talking about video games—an interest of his—he could not find a good way to integrate himself into the conversation. As Zane describes, he didn't know how to start the conversation, he was not making good eye contact ("I was staring at the floor"), he was providing more information than necessary without incorporating the perspectives of the other children ("I started talking about all the things I knew about the game"), he was unable to demonstrate appropriate speech and language skills, and he showed poor problem-solving abilities in this particular situation ("When the other kids walked away, I started talking louder"). What Zane demonstrated here are the main symptoms that are common to ASD: impairments in social communication and social interaction.

Good social functioning requires us to simultaneously process what is said by others; the type of language used; the intonation, volume, and rhythm of speech; gestures and body language such as head nods, eyebrow raises, arm and hand movements, and facial expressions; and the environment or setting. We also have to take into consideration what the other person may be thinking and put ourselves in his or her shoes—in other words, demonstrate good perspective taking. If we fail to do any one of those things, our ability to fully understand the social exchange may be limited. There are so many factors that go into a particular social interaction which dictate the entire meaning of what has been said. Take sarcasm, for instance. Someone stating, "That is real nice, Charlie," with an emphasis on the "real nice" and a scowl on their face means something completely different than someone stating, "That is real nice, Charlie," with a kind tone and a smile on their face.

Zane likely had difficulty picking up on the nuances in this conversation. In addition, Zane experienced challenges with problem-solving in this situation, particularly with regard to his ability to react flexibly and "in the moment." Challenges in thinking flexibly—or what is known as "shifting-set"—is also a common weakness in

children with ASD. Zane couldn't shift, or move on, when the situation demanded a change in behavior. Instead, Zane decided to talk louder in an effort to get his peers to pay attention to him. Zane was hoping this would help him stay involved in the conversation, but instead likely made his peers irritated with his behavior as they were trying to get ready for science class. Zane was trying to reach out to his peers, but his attempts were actually self-defeating. This can make kids with ASD feel frustrated and confused.

Literal and Concrete Thinking Styles: "Whatever floats your boat"

Zane feels different because of his tendency to think concretely and literally. Literal thinking and difficulty deciphering idioms or figures of speech, such as "you're pulling my leg," are common in kids with ASD. Figures of speech have a literal meaning and a figurative meaning, and some kids with ASD tend to take these kinds of statements quite literally. Unfortunately for individuals like Zane, this way of communicating is quite common in our culture. Think of phrases such as, "He has a chip on his shoulder," "That's just a drop in the bucket," "Oh no! You spilled the beans," "That jacket costs an arm and a leg," and "That should have been a piece of cake for you." These types of language patterns are woven throughout our day-to-day interactions and even used to explain academic subjects or define classroom expectations. For some kids with ASD, this can make the world more challenging and frustrating to navigate. Being aware of your use of these phrases—and providing interpretations when you use them—can be an important way to help your child navigate these communication challenges.

Individual Strengths: "When I look at you, I see many different stripes"

Like everyone else in this world, Zane has his own individual strengths and weaknesses. ASD is considered a "spectrum" because there are such varied individual differences among these strengths and weaknesses. Zane's mother points out the many "stripes" that denote Zane's strengths. As Zane's mother points out, Zane has a "pilot stripe," which is also called visual memory. Some, though not all, children with ASD have exceptional memories for certain types of information or interests (e.g., animal kingdoms, video games, cartoons, subway lines, or dates of historical events). However, some children with ASD may have poorer memories relative to their peers for things such as turning in homework, remembering to shake someone's hand and make eye contact when greeting or departing, or recalling that their peers do not like to talk continuously about certain games or topics.

In addition, Zane's mother loves his "caring stripe." It is a common misconception that children with ASD are not able to express themselves or understand the emotions of others. It may be a relative weakness for some, and they may have periodic challenges with deciphering what someone else may be feeling, but it is completely inaccurate to say children with ASD are unable to do so. Similarly, someone may struggle with math, or even have a specific learning disorder, but it doesn't mean that person is unable to complete math problems or understand math concepts. It simply means he may need additional supports, time, and understanding in accomplishing certain tasks in particular contexts. As the story appropriately demonstrates, Zane is kind, caring, and able to stand up for others. He is an emotional being who frequently enjoys interacting with the world and other people.

Finally, Zane is honest and loves to learn. Sometimes challenges associated with literal or concrete thinking patterns can also come with a refreshing and welcome dose of honesty. This may not only provide some much needed comic relief (e.g., "Mom, I think your new hat is ugly"), but these characteristics can be good behaviors for children with ASD to model for their peers who may struggle in this arena. Furthermore, children with ASD can exhibit well-developed cognitive and academic skill sets. With the appropriate supports in place, many children on the autism spectrum can perform well within the classroom setting, far above their "neurotypical" peers.

ASD are a set of neurodevelopmental syndromes that come with both an array of challenges, and even more importantly, strengths. To reiterate, and as Zane demonstrates in the story, children with ASD often understand, process, and interact with the world differently: sometimes in ways that make life better, sometimes in ways that make life more challenging, and sometimes just simply in ways that make them wonderfully unique.

Note to Parents and Caregivers

by Drew C. Coman, PhD, and Ellen Braaten, PhD

Autism spectrum disorder (ASD) is the term that is now used for a group of disorders formerly referred to as autistic disorder, Asperger's syndrome, and pervasive developmental disorder, not otherwise specified (PDD-NOS). While these terms may still at times be used by families and professionals, the term ASD is thought to best represent the vast individual differences in symptoms among those affected by this disorder. The hallmark symptoms of ASD include: challenges in social communication (both verbal and nonverbal), challenges in social interaction (the ability to cultivate and maintain friendships), and restricted, repetitive patterns of behavior, interests, or activities (such as sensory challenges, fixated and intense interests, a "need" for strict routines, and repetitive or odd motor movements). The severity and frequency of these symptoms can vary considerably. Each individual affected has different strengths and weaknesses, and a unique overall profile. In fact, professionals who specialize in ASD frequently comment, "When you've worked with one child on the autism spectrum, you've worked with one child on the autism spectrum." That is precisely why it is called a spectrum, defined as a condition that is not restricted to a specific set of values but can differ infinitely along continuums. In this case, these continuums can include, but are not limited to, social, language, behavioral, sensory, cognitive, and emotional functioning. *All My Stripes* portrays Zane's specific profile of strengths and weaknesses, some of which may resonate with your family or students and some which may not. Nevertheless it highlights some of the most common challenges faced by children affected by ASD. Just as importantly, it gives insight into the many strengths children with ASD exhibit, which should not be overlooked.

How This Book Can Help

All My Stripes provides readers a small yet enlightening glimpse into a day in the life of a young, smart, caring, honest, and curious zebra named Zane. Zane is experiencing challenges at school often associated with ASD. This story can serve as a teaching tool for caregivers—such as parents, grandparents, and teachers—to help other children and family members understand the various challenges individuals on the autism spectrum face on a day-to-day basis. Those that are highlighted in this story are discussed in more depth in the Reading Guide.

What Might Symptoms of Autism Spectrum Disorders Look Like?

It is important to note that any one, or even several, of the symptoms listed below do not warrant a diagnosis of ASD. *A formal clinical evaluation by an appropriately credentialed clinician is necessary for a diagnosis of ASD.* Additionally, some of these behaviors can be associated with other developmental challenges, and some of these symptoms can be entirely developmentally typical. These are simply signs that may warrant follow-up with your primary care provider.

EARLY CHILDHOOD: AGES 2–5 YEARS

ASD can typically be reliably diagnosed by 24 months. Early signs of ASD include:

- Poor or inconsistent eye contact when playing with or interacting with others.
- Speech and language difficulties and/or the use of language that seems strange, including significant speech delays, repeatedly using a phrase with a peculiar or "sing-songy"

tone, pronoun reversals (e.g., referring to themselves as "he," "she," or "you"), unusual volume or mechanical speech (e.g., speech that is overly formal or "robot-like"), poor or inconsistent response to others calling their name, and immediate repetition of words or phrases they hear—"parroting" TV shows or phrases from others.

- Few attempts to interact with others and/or odd attempts to engage others, either verbally or nonverbally, such as the use of another person's body as a tool to play with a toy or open a door, or grabbing another's face to have them look at something.
- Challenges interacting with friends or peers at daycare or preschool.
- Minimal use of gestures, such as pointing or describing things with their hands (e.g., saying the truck was so "big" while opening their arms wide).
- Not showing facial expressions to direct emotion or providing expressions that do not match the circumstance.
- Not pointing to shift another's attention to objects across the room or setting, such as a plane in the sky, a dog across the park, or their juice box on the counter.
- Not showing objects to others, such as an empty sippy-cup, their red truck or doll, an acorn found on the ground, or a new toy that their mom or dad just brought home.
- Challenges with responding to or following the eyes and facial expressions of others who are attempting to get them to look at an object across the room. For example, children with ASD may be unable to make eye contact with a parent and follow his or her gaze and vocal attempts to get them to look at an object.
- Not smiling in response to parents' or familiar adults' smiles.
- Limited displays of enjoyment or interest in social games like peek-a-boo or tickle games.
- Poor imaginative play or "play" that consists of lining up toys, organizing toys in a certain order or fashion, or other behaviors that appear strange.

- Frequent sensory-seeking behaviors or odd repetitive motor mannerisms, such as hand flapping, spinning, walking on toes, or looking at objects in a peculiar fashion through the corner of their eye.
- Over-sensitivity to noises, touch, smells, or specific stimuli.
- Intense or unusually repetitive interests in objects (e.g., toilets, maps, trains) that gets in the way of them interacting with others or their environment.
- Difficulties with changes in routine and adherence to particular routines.

OLDER CHILDREN: AGES 5–9 YEARS

Symptoms of ASD may change across the course of development. As children with ASD get older and mature, they may no longer exhibit some of the symptoms they evidenced early on. Additionally, some of those symptoms may evolve into a much different presentation. This may be particularly true for children who have received intensive, early intervention. However, even in children who have received intervention—and especially in those who have not—new symptoms may emerge. In addition to the symptoms noted above, common ASD symptoms in the school-aged years may include the following:

- Continued challenges with poor or inconsistent eye contact, even when someone is directly speaking to them.
- Challenges with having a conversation, such as difficulties with organizing their thoughts or words, saying things (possibly involving an intense interest of their own) inappropriate to the conversation topic, or challenges with giving a step-by-step account of events, such as a recent family vacation.
- Limited use of gesturing while communicating with others—such as using hands to describe the shape or size of an object, pointing, or using fingers to indicate the number of objects.
- Continued challenges with initiating, establishing, and maintaining social relationships

with their same-aged peers.

- Excessive or repetitive interests in topics, objects, or content to the extent that it gets in the way of successful social interactions with others.
- Challenges with executive functioning, which includes staying on task, planning, time management, sustained and shifting attention, organization of materials, and efficient (i.e., quick and accurate) thinking abilities.
- Related to challenges in executive functioning are difficulties with emotion regulation (e.g., outbursts, symptoms of anxiety or depression, or poor self-esteem). Children on the autism spectrum often have difficulty with regulating their emotional states, which can be a result of several factors, including but not limited to sensory difficulties, chronic negative feedback from others in social situations, challenges with understanding the social world, and the social world understanding them, and/or a need for structure and predictability.
- Children with ASD can also experience academic difficulties in the areas of reading comprehension, math, writing, and any subject areas that require "big-picture" thinking, making connections between concepts, or inferencing.

What Can I Do as a Caregiver?

The following are some strategies to help you further understand ASD and locate necessary supports and services for your child.

Get your child screened, and if warranted, get a formal evaluation.

Early detection and early intervention are essential. First, your pediatrician should be conducting screenings for ASD—if your pediatrician is not, request that he or she do so. There are several quick but scientifically-backed measures used to screen for ASD, and helpful resources can be found at the Centers for Disease Control and Prevention's website, available at http://www. cdc.gov/ncbddd/autism/screening.html. Next, if

screening indicates some concern(s), having your child formally evaluated will assist in confirming ASD-related challenges and identifying his or her profile of strengths and weaknesses, which will set the groundwork for essential interventions and services.

Get your child enrolled into treatment.

It is essential that treatments are individualized and tailored to your child and family. It is also vital that your family's resources are used for services that have been supported by research. For information about validated, research-based, empirically supported treatments and interventions for ASD, parents are encouraged to visit the recent National Standards Project publication, available at http://www.nationalautismcenter .org/nsp/reports.php. These treatments may include, but are not limited to, the following home, clinic, and school-based services:

- Applied-Behavior Analysis (ABA) therapy—a therapeutic approach that shapes and reinforces new behaviors, such as learning to talk or interact with others, and reduces problematic behaviors.
- Speech and language therapy—an intervention that assesses and treats speech, language, and communication problems in order to help your child communicate.
- Occupational therapy—a service that promotes children's abilities to perform day-to-day activities (e.g., feeding, dressing), assists with gross (e.g., balance) and fine (e.g., using a pencil) coordination and strength, and ameliorates challenges associated with sensory processing issues.
- Social skills training—an intervention that promotes children's understanding of how to effectively engage in social settings with peers and adults.
- Executive functioning training—a service geared towards, but not limited to, helping children with organizational skills, study strategies, time management, and task initiation and completion.

- Academic tutoring—a service aimed at promoting children's learning in specific academic areas (e.g., reading, writing, spelling, math, etc.).
- Access to necessary medical professionals (e.g., psychiatrists, neurologists, gastroenterologists, etc.).
- Individual therapy and/or parent training if emotional concerns arise.

There are various avenues for finding these different types of treatment. First, parents are encouraged to discuss with the professional that evaluated their child and recommended these services as to how they might access local agencies and clinics that provide these interventions. Families should also seek access to these treatments with the help of their pediatrician, as well as through the school system by contacting the special education department at their child's school. Additionally, parents and caregivers can also contact any one or all of these national organizations for assistance in accessing local agencies and treatment facilities:

- Autism Science Foundation (www.autismsciencefoundation.org)
- Autism Society of America (www.autism-society.org)
- National Autism Association (www.nationalautismassociation.org)
- U.S. Autism and Asperger Association (www.usautism.org)

Follow up about your child's progress.

As your child matures, and expectations at home and school change, regular evaluations either privately or within the school setting are essential to ensure progress is being made with the services and therapies that have been put into place.

Seek out supports at school.

Several of the interventions listed above are often (not always) available through your child's school system, including ABA, speech and language therapy, social skills training, occupational therapy, access to a school psychologist or counselor, individual academic tutoring, and executive functioning assistance. Families are encouraged to contact the special education department at their child's school for a better understanding of the available services. Your child's school-based services should be geared towards promoting all of the following areas: academic, social, emotional, language, and adaptive development.

Keep the lines of communication open.

Close communication between your child's school administration, teachers, medical providers, mental health providers, and your family is extremely important. For one, the nature of children's learning, emotional, and social difficulties tends to change because they require different functions to perform effectively at different ages. Furthermore, evolving subject matter in school calls for different capacities in different grades. Therefore, families want to ensure progress is being made with the services and therapies that have been put into place. Additionally, communication between your child's team of providers is one of the most important ingredients for addressing your child's needs. For example, both medical and mental health providers can provide school personnel with key strategies related to how your child learns, processes information, and copes with stress, and what classroom environments are ideal.

Take the time to take care of yourself.

Parents and caregivers of children with ASD are at increased risk for emotional distress relative to parents of "neurotypical" children as well as parents of children with other disorders. The national organizations that are listed above can be helpful resources for finding local parent support groups. Additionally, families are encouraged to become active members of local agencies and/or chapters that support ASD. These organizations often provide conferences, family outings, and benefits such as walks to raise awareness about ASD. Furthermore, it is essential that you find the time to do activities that relax you: for example, take vacations with or without family members, exercise, join a book club, go to dinner with your loved ones without kids, have periodic "ladies'" or "guys'" nights out, or enroll in a yoga class. Your child will greatly benefit from you feeling good about you.

Early detection and early intervention are essential for children and families affected by ASD. Again, a formal clinical evaluation by a professional is imperative in getting an accurate diagnosis and recommendations for treatment. However, with this evaluation at the helm, there are effective treatments available for children and currently a vast array of research is being conducted to discover even more interventions. We hope you find this information helpful in further understanding ASD and accessing the appropriate services if needed. Remember that you are not in this alone: help is available to you and your family.

DREW COMAN, PHD, is a staff psychologist at the Learning and Emotional Assessment Program (LEAP) at Massachusetts General Hospital (MGH). Dr. Coman completed his training at the University of Miami and MGH/Harvard Medical School. He conducts research on autism spectrum disorders (ASD) and specializes in neuropsychological assessments of children and adolescents affected by ASD and other comorbid conditions.

ELLEN BRAATEN, PHD, is the director of the Learning and Emotional Assessment Program (LEAP) at Massachusetts General Hospital and assistant professor of psychology at Harvard Medical School. She is also the coauthor of *Straight Talk about Psychological Testing for Kids* and *Bright Kids Who Can't Keep Up*.

About the Authors

SHAINA RUDOLPH has been educating children in urban and suburban settings for 12 years. Working in different socioeconomic environments has allowed her the rare capability to develop close relationships with students from all walks of life. These relationships, in turn, have taught her the importance of reaching one's potential. She instills this belief daily in her students while she works as a reading specialist with children who have learning differences in the greater Los Angeles area.

DANIELLE ROYER has had a passion for teaching and working with children from a young age. Inspired by her two youngest brothers, both of whom have learning differences, she has always felt it extremely important that children feel comfortable and empowered in their own skin. Over her career, she has cultivated this message of empowerment to cater to her students' individual needs, no matter their stripes. She continues to spread her message and educate children in Santa Monica, CA.

About the Illustrator

JENNIFER ZIVOIN has always loved art and storytelling, so becoming an illustrator was a natural career path. She has been trained in media ranging from figure drawing to virtual reality, and earned her bachelor of arts degree with highest distinction from the honors division of Indiana University. During her professional career, Jennifer worked as a graphic designer and then as a creative director before finding her artistic niche illustrating children's books. In addition to artwork, she enjoys reading, cooking, and ballroom dancing. Jennifer lives in Indiana with her family.

About Magination Press

MAGINATION PRESS is an imprint of the American Psychological Association, the largest scientific and professional organization representing psychologists in the United States and the largest association of psychologists worldwide.